SCIENCE AT WORK

TEMPERATURE

AT

WORK

LAUREN KUKLA

Consulting Editor, Diane Craig, M.A./Reading Specialist

Sandcastle

An Imprint of Abdo Publishing
abdopublishing.com

abdopublishing.com

Published by Abdo Publishing, a division of ABDO, PO Box 398166, Minneapolis, Minnesota 55439. Copyright © 2017 by Abdo Consulting Group, Inc. International copyrights reserved in all countries. No part of this book may be reproduced in any form without written permission from the publisher. SandCastle™ is a trademark and logo of Abdo Publishing.

Printed in the United States of America, North Mankato, Minnesota

062016
092016

THIS BOOK CONTAINS
RECYCLED MATERIALS

Design: Mighty Media, Inc.
Content Developer: Nancy Tuminelly
Production: Mighty Media, Inc.
Editor: Liz Salzmann
Photo Credits: Shutterstock, Wikimedia Commons

Library of Congress Cataloging-in-Publication Data

Names: Kukla, Lauren, author.
Title: Temperature at work / Lauren Kukla ; consulting editor, Diane Craig, M.A./reading specialist.
Description: Minneapolis, Minnesota : Abdo Publishing, [2017] | Series: Science at work
Identifiers: LCCN 2016000313 (print) | LCCN 2016010747 (ebook) | ISBN 9781680781441 (print) | ISBN 9781680775877 (ebook)
Subjects: LCSH: Temperature--Juvenile literature.
Classification: LCC QC271.4 .K85 2017 (print) | LCC QC271.4 (ebook) | DDC 536/.5--dc23
LC record available at http://lccn.loc.gov/2016000313

SandCastle™ Level: Fluent

SandCastle™ books are created by a team of professional educators, reading specialists, and content developers around five essential components—phonemic awareness, phonics, vocabulary, text comprehension, and fluency—to assist young readers as they develop reading skills and strategies and increase their general knowledge. All books are written, reviewed, and leveled for guided reading, early reading intervention, and Accelerated Reader™ programs for use in shared, guided, and independent reading and writing activities to support a balanced approach to literacy instruction. The SandCastle™ series has four levels that correspond to early literacy development. The levels are provided to help teachers and parents select appropriate books for young readers.

EMERGING · BEGINNING · TRANSITIONAL · FLUENT

CONTENTS

ABOUT TEMPERATURE

Have you ever watched ice melt? Or felt steam rising out of a hot **chocolate**?

This was
temperature
at work!

Temperature is how hot or cold
something is. Thermometers
measure temperature.

Jay takes his temperature.

Heat is a kind of **energy**. It comes from **molecules**. These are very tiny.

Everything is made of **molecules**.

Molecules can move very fast.
This gives off **energy**.

The **energy** is heat.

Molecules can move slowly.
Then there is less **energy**.

The object cools down.

Temperature can cause something to change. Water **freezes** when it is cold.

It turns to steam when it is hot.

Many scientists have studied temperature. Daniel Gabriel Fahrenheit invented a scale.

It measures temperature.
The United States uses his scale.

Anders Celsius made a different scale.
Many other countries use his scale.

Nora sees that it is cold outside.
She wears a coat.

Kyle knows it is a warm
day. He wears a T-shirt.

THINK ABOUT IT

Look around you! Where else is
temperature at work?

TUE
39 °F

W

S
4

How do
you use it?

GLOSSARY

chocolate – a food made from cacao beans. Sweets such as candy and cake are often flavored with chocolate.

energy – a natural power that can affect other things.

freeze – to become solid ice from being in the cold.

molecule – a group of two or more atoms that make up the smallest piece of a substance.